IN THE CITY OF VARANASI, A YOUNG MAN WAS ONCE ON THE LOOK-OUT FOR A JOB.

IT SO HAPPENED THAT THE ROYAL TREASURER, ACCOMPANIED BY A FRIEND, PASSED BY.

THE KING VALUES YOUR WORK. THE TREASURY IS OVERFLOWING WITH RICHES. WHAT IS THE SECRET OF YOUR SUCCESS?

INITIATIVE AND ENTERPRISE.

I'LL EXPLAIN WHAT I MEAN. DO YOU SEE THAT DEAD MOUSE?

YES... BUT....

EVEN IF HE HAS NO MONEY, A YOUNG MAN WITH INITIATIVE COULD JUST PICK UP THAT MOUSE AND START A BUSINESS.

A DEAD MOUSE AS CAPITAL? HA! HA! HA!

THE YOUNG MAN STOPPED AND GAZED AT THE DEAD MOUSE.

IT SOUNDS LIKE AN ABSURD IDEA...

... BUT THE TREASURER MUST SURELY KNOW WHAT HE IS TALKING ABOUT!

BUT WHAT CAN I DO WITH IT?

WHO WOULD WANT TO BUY A DEAD MOUSE?

HEY, PUSSY, COME BACK!

OH! I'VE GOT IT. I MUST FIND OUT IF THERE IS A DEMAND FOR SOMETHING AND THEN ARRANGE TO SUPPLY IT!

PLEASE GIVE ME ONE PAISA'S WORTH OF GUR.

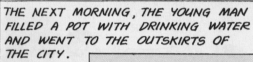

THE NEXT MORNING, THE YOUNG MAN FILLED A POT WITH DRINKING WATER AND WENT TO THE OUTSKIRTS OF THE CITY.

I'LL WAIT HERE FOR THE FLOWER-GATHERERS TO RETURN FROM WORK.

IN THE FOREST, WORKERS WERE BUSY COLLECTING FLOWERS.

IT WAS LATE IN THE AFTERNOON WHEN THEY FINISHED THEIR WORK AND BEGAN RETURNING TO THE CITY.

IT'S SO HOT! AND I'M SO THIRSTY!

THERE WON'T BE ANY WATER TO DRINK TILL WE REACH THE CITY

AH! HERE THEY COME!

BROTHER, YOU MUST BE TIRED. HAVE SOME WATER AND A LITTLE GUR.

THANK YOU, SON. MAY YOU LIVE LONG.

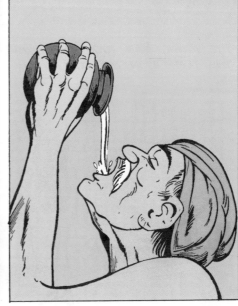

5

ALL I CAN GIVE YOU...

...IS THIS BUNCH OF FLOWERS.

THANK YOU, UNCLE.

HOW REFRESHED WE FEEL AFTER DRINKING THAT WATER! MAY THESE FLOWERS ALSO MAKE YOU HAPPY, SON.

THANK YOU.

EACH OF THE WORKERS DRANK SOME WATER AND GAVE HIM A BUNCH OF FLOWERS IN RETURN.

BRING US WATER TOMORROW AS WELL, MY FRIEND.

I WILL.

THE YOUNG MAN TOOK THE FLOWERS TO THE TEMPLE IN THE CITY.

THERE HE SOLD THEM.

HERE IS THE MONEY.

IN A MINUTE, SIR.

A BUNCH FOR ME, TOO.

NOW I HAVE EIGHT COPPER PIECES.

WITH THE MONEY HE EARNED, THE YOUNG MAN BOUGHT A BIG WATER POT AND A LARGER QUANTITY OF GUR. THE NEXT DAY HE WENT BACK TO THE FOREST.

TODAY YOU MAY HAVE A LITTLE MORE GUR.

MAY GOD BLESS YOU, SON.

LATER, HE WENT EVEN FURTHER AWAY, TO THE FIELDS WHERE GRASS-CUTTERS WERE WORKING.

IS ANYBODY THIRSTY?

YOU WON'T FIND ANYONE HERE WHO IS NOT THIRSTY. GIVE ME SOME WATER, SON.

BROTHER, YOU ARE KIND TO US. WHAT CAN WE DO FOR YOU IN RETURN?

NOTHING AT PRESENT.

BUT DON'T HESITATE TO ASK US WHEN YOU NEED OUR HELP.

A MONTH PASSED BY. ONE EVENING, THE YOUNG MAN WAS RETURNING HOME, WHEN A STORM BROKE OUT.

EVERYWHERE, THE WIND BLEW DOWN LEAVES AND DRY BRANCHES.

IF THERE IS MONEY IN A DEAD MOUSE THERE SHOULD BE MONEY IN THESE LEAVES AND BRANCHES, TOO!

THE NEXT MORNING HE WENT TO THE PALACE GARDEN AND SPOKE TO THE GARDENER.

YOU LOOK WORRIED, UNCLE. CAN I HELP YOU?

HOW CAN YOU? THE GARDEN IS LITTERED WITH BRANCHES...

...AND THE KING IS EXPECTED ANY MOMENT NOW. I DON'T KNOW HOW TO CLEAR THE MESS BEFORE HE COMES.

I'LL HELP YOU IF I CAN KEEP THE FALLEN BRANCHES.

TAKE THEM, SON. ONLY, TAKE THEM AWAY SOON.

I'LL GO AND GET SOME HELP. I'LL BE BACK IN A MINUTE.

THE YOUNG MAN DID NOT HAVE TO GO FAR —

WOULD YOU LIKE TO HAVE SOME GUR?

GUR! OH, CERTAINLY!

JUST AS THE YOUNG MAN WAS WONDERING WHAT HE SHOULD DO NEXT...

...A POTTER CAME BY AND STOPPED HIS CART.

IS THAT FOR SALE?

YES!

HERE ARE SIXTEEN COPPER PIECES. PLEASE HELP ME LOAD MY CART.

YES, OF COURSE!

NOW I HAVE ALL THE WOOD I NEED TO FIRE THE POTS SPECIALLY ORDERED BY THE KING.

THE YOUNG MAN THEN WENT WITH THE POTTER...

...TO THE MARKET.

HAVE YOU HEARD? THE HORSE-DEALER WILL BE COMING TOMORROW.

YES, YES. I HEAR HE WILL BE BRINGING FIVE HUNDRED HORSES TO SELL.

AH, HA! THAT'S USEFUL INFORMATION! THANKS FOR LETTING ME KNOW!

HURRIEDLY, HE WENT TO THE GRASS-CUTTERS.

FRIENDS, I SEEK A FAVOUR OF YOU.

AT LAST! TELL US WHAT WE SHOULD DO.

I WANT A BUNDLE OF GRASS FROM EACH OF YOU.

WE ARE FIVE HUNDRED IN ALL — SO AS MANY BUNDLES OF GRASS WILL BE DELIVERED TO YOU TONIGHT.

AND I WANT YOU TO PROMISE THAT TILL TOMORROW AFTERNOON YOU WILL NOT SELL ANYONE ANY GRASS AT ALL.

YOU ARE OUR FRIEND. AND WE WILL DO WHAT YOU ASK WITHOUT QUESTION.

LATE THAT EVENING —

YOU SEE, WE HAVE KEPT OUR WORD!

I SHALL BE FOREVER INDEBTED TO YOU.

THE NEXT MORNING THE HORSE-DEALER ARRIVED WITH FIVE HUNDRED HORSES AT THE OUTSKIRTS OF VARANASI.

STRANGE! NO ONE HAS COME YET TO SELL ME GRASS FOR MY HORSES.

HE WENT TO THE MARKET.

NO GRASS IN VARANASI?

WHERE HAVE THE GRASS-CUTTERS GONE? I'D BETTER GO FURTHER— NEARER THE FIELDS.

GRASS! AT LAST!

A DAY LATER —

WHY IS IT SO QUIET HERE TODAY? IS ANYTHING THE MATTER?

EVERYONE IS AWAY MAKING PREPARATIONS TO RECEIVE THE BOATS THAT WILL BE ARRIVING TOMORROW.

BOATS... ARRIVING TOMORROW?

AN IDEA STRUCK HIM LIKE LIGHTNING —

HE BOUGHT NEW CLOTHES AND THEN WENT TO HIRE A CARRIAGE.

SEND THE CARRIAGE TO ME EARLY TOMORROW MORNING. HERE IS SOME MONEY AS AN ADVANCE.

VERY EARLY THE NEXT MORNING THE YOUNG MAN RODE IN STYLE TO THE RIVER HARBOUR WITH TWO FRIENDS...

...AND WAITED TO RECEIVE THE VISITING MERCHANT.

HE WAS, NATURALLY, THE FIRST TO GREET THE MERCHANT.

WELCOME TO VARANASI!

I AM HAPPY TO MEET YOU, SIR.

I WANT TO BUY ALL THE MERCHANDISE YOU HAVE BROUGHT.

RIGHT. IT IS A PLEASURE TO DO BUSINESS WITH YOU.

THE MERCHANT QUOTED A PRICE TO WHICH THE YOUNG MAN READILY AGREED.

I NEED TIME TO ARRANGE THE PAYMENT. MEANWHILE, HERE IS MY SIGNET RING AS SECURITY.

THEN THE YOUNG MAN SET UP A CANVAS SHELTER AND WAITED —

WHEN THE CITY MERCHANTS COME, BRING THEM IN WITH DUE COURTESY.

AT DAYBREAK, A HUNDRED MERCHANTS CAME TO THE HARBOUR.

MY FRIEND, WE HAVE COME TO DO BUSINESS WITH YOU!

I'M SORRY, SIR. I HAVE ALREADY SOLD EVERYTHING.

SOLD EVERYTHING! WHEN? TO WHOM?

TO THAT YOUNG MERCHANT OVER THERE.

HE IS NOT ONE OF US!

WE CAN'T LET ANY NEW PERSONS INTO OUR TRADE —OR WE'LL BE RUINED!

THAT WILL MAKE IT A HUNDRED THOUSAND PIECES SINCE THERE ARE A HUNDRED MERCHANTS HERE!

... MOREOVER, WE'D LIKE TO BUY YOUR SHARE IN IT TOO.

NO! NO!

BUT WE'LL PAY HANDSOMELY — ONE THOUSAND PIECES EACH.

THAT WILL MAKE IT ANOTHER HUNDRED THOUSAND GOLD PIECES!

HAVING AGREED TO THE DEAL, THE YOUNG MAN RETURNED HOME —

I WILL STILL HAVE A BIG AMOUNT LEFT AFTER PAYING THE MERCHANT. AND I OWE IT ALL TO THE TREASURER'S WISDOM!

TO SHOW HIS GRATITUDE, HE WENT TO CALL ON THE TREASURER, TAKING HALF HIS PROFITS WITH HIM.

SIR, PERMIT ME TO PRESENT YOU WITH THESE COINS AS MY HUMBLE GURU-DAKSHINA.

GURU-DAKSHINA!

BUT I HAVEN'T SEEN YOU BEFORE! I HAVEN'T TAUGHT YOU ANYTHING!

YES, YOU HAVE! I CAME BY ALL MY WEALTH IN FOUR SHORT MONTHS, SIMPLY BY FOLLOWING YOUR TEACHING.

THEN HE TOLD THE TREASURER THE WHOLE STORY, STARTING WITH THE DEAD MOUSE —

THIS YOUNG MAN IS EXTRAORDINARILY CLEVER —JUST THE PERSON I'D CHOOSE FOR MY LOVELY DAUGHTER.

SO HE MARRIED THE YOUNG MAN TO HIS DAUGHTER AND GAVE HIM ALL HIS FAMILY ESTATES.

THE GODDESS OF SUCCESS SMILES ON THOSE WHO SHOW INITIATIVE. MAY YOU ALWAYS BE SO FORTUNATE, MY SON!

THE INVALUABLE TREASURE

IN VARANASI, THERE ONCE LIVED A WATER-CARRIER.

THOUGH HE WORKED HARD, HE BARELY EARNED ENOUGH FOR TWO MEALS A DAY.

HOWEVER, ONE DAY HE MADE A LITTLE EXTRA MONEY.

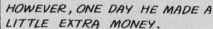

ONE PAISA!

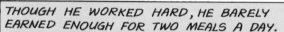

BUT WHERE SHALL I HIDE MY TREASURE?

IT WILL BE SAFE BEHIND ONE OF THESE BRICKS.

HE BEGAN GENTLY TO TAP AT THE BRICKS.

AH! I THINK I'VE FOUND A LOOSE BRICK!

IT'S THE FIRST BRICK TO THE LEFT OF THE NORTHERN GATE...

...AND THE TENTH ONE FROM THE GROUND LEVEL.

THE PLACE WILL BE EASY TO REMEMBER.

THAT WAS THE ONLY TIME HE HAD EARNED A LITTLE MORE THAN HE ABSOLUTELY NEEDED. HE HAD NEVER HAD SUCH LUCK BEFORE.

AH! MY TREASURE IS SAFE THERE. I AM A RICH MAN!

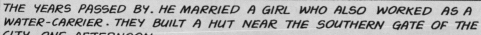

THE YEARS PASSED BY. HE MARRIED A GIRL WHO ALSO WORKED AS A WATER-CARRIER. THEY BUILT A HUT NEAR THE SOUTHERN GATE OF THE CITY. ONE AFTERNOON —

I WISH WE COULD GO TO TOWN THIS EVENING TO ATTEND THE FAIR! BUT WE DON'T HAVE ENOUGH MONEY.

OF COURSE, WE DO! I HAVE MONEY — ONE PAISA! I'VE HIDDEN IT AWAY IN A SAFE PLACE.

I, TOO, HAVE ONE PAISA. IF YOU'LL BRING YOURS, WE'LL HAVE ENOUGH TO ENJOY OURSELVES.

I WILL GO NOW AND BRING YOU MY TREASURE.

COME BACK SOON!

YES, YES, I'LL BE BACK AT ONCE!

24

IT WAS SUMMER. THE MIDDAY SUN WAS BLAZING IN THE SKY. NO ONE WAS TO BE SEEN ON THE STREETS EXCEPT THE WATER-CARRIER WHO WAS RUNNING WITH A SONG ON HIS LIPS.

AH! THERE'S THE PLACE! ONLY A LITTLE MORE DISTANCE TO GO!

KING UDAYA, WHO WAS RELAXING IN THE PALACE BALCONY, SAW THE WATER-CARRIER.

I WONDER WHAT MAKES HIM RUN AT THIS TIME OF THE DAY, LOOKING SO HAPPY!

HE SENT WORD TO HAVE THE MAN BROUGHT TO HIM —

HEY! STOP!

LET ME GO!

THE KING WANTS TO SPEAK TO YOU. COME!

I HAVE MORE IMPORTANT THINGS TO DO. I HAVE NO TIME TO MEET THE KING ....

WHAT A SIMPLE MAN! DON'T YOU REALISE IT IS AN HONOUR TO BE TAKEN BEFORE THE KING?

THE GUARDS HAD TO USE FORCE TO TAKE THE WATER-CARRIER TO THE KING.

THE KING ASKED IF IT WERE A THOUSAND, A HUNDRED, FIFTY, TEN GOLD COINS. BUT THE WATER-CARRIER SHOOK HIS HEAD —

NO, NO. NOT THAT MUCH!

THEN HOW MUCH IS IT?

IT IS ONE PAISA, MY KING.

ONE PAISA!

YES, WITH THAT MONEY I CAN BUY A LOT OF THINGS FOR MY WIFE AND MAKE HER HAPPY.

MY FRIEND, YOU DON'T HAVE TO RUN TO THE NORTHERN GATE TO GET ONE PAISA. I WILL GIVE IT TO YOU.

HERE, TAKE THIS AND GO HOME.

I WILL TAKE WHAT YOU GIVE ME. BUT I WILL GO AND GET THE OTHER COIN, TOO.

MY FRIEND, DON'T EXERT YOURSELF. I WILL GIVE YOU TWO PAISAS.

I WILL ACCEPT THEM. ALL THE SAME, I WILL GET THE OTHER ONE, TOO.

I WILL GIVE YOU TEN. PLEASE RETURN HOME.

I'LL TAKE TEN— BUT THE OTHER ONE, TOO.

HE IS SO ATTACHED TO THE ONE PAISA HE HAS SAVED! BUT POOR MAN! HE'LL HAVE TO RUN ALL THE WAY TO THE NORTHERN GATE TO GET IT!

THE KING RAISED HIS OFFER.

I WILL GIVE YOU A HUNDRED PAISAS.

A THOUSAND!

TEN THOUSAND!

THANK YOU. I WILL TAKE ALL YOU OFFER— AND THE ONE I HAVE HIDDEN, TOO.

IS THERE NO WAY I CAN SAVE HIM FROM THIS STUBBORNNESS?

DESPERATELY, THE KING RAISED HIS OFFER AGAIN AND AGAIN. BUT THE WATER-CARRIER INSISTED THAT HE WOULD GO AND FETCH HIS HIDDEN TREASURE. FINALLY —

I WILL GIVE YOU HALF MY KINGDOM IF ONLY YOU WILL AGREE TO DROP THE IDEA OF RUNNING NOW FOR ONE PAISA!

I AGREE!

AT LAST! I AM HAPPY TO HAVE YOUR AGREEMENT!

THE KING HELD A DARBAR TO CROWN THE WATER-CARRIER KING OF ONE HALF OF THE KINGDOM.

NOW, FRIEND, TELL ME WHICH HALF OF THE KINGDOM YOU CHOOSE TO HAVE.

THE WATER-CARRIER THOUGHT FOR A SECOND —

I WANT THE NORTHERN HALF OF THE KINGDOM.

YOU'VE WON AGAIN!

THUS, THE WATER-CARRIER NOT ONLY GOT HALF THE KINGDOM BUT ALSO HIS TREASURE WHICH WAS HIDDEN IN THE NORTHERN WALL.

THE RIGHT MOMENT

KING SUVARNAKA WAS A GENEROUS MONARCH. NO SUPPLICANT EVER LEFT WITHOUT RECEIVING A GIFT FROM HIM...

...EXCEPT YASHOVARMAN.

I DO WISH TO GIVE YOU GIFTS. BUT THE SUN GOD PREVENTS ME FROM DOING SO.

AS LONG AS HE IS WATCHING, I CANNOT GRATIFY YOUR WISH.

ONLY TWO CATEGORIES OF PEOPLE DESERVE GIFTS — THE OLD AND INFIRM OR THE PANDITS.

HE IS NOT INFIRM. SO LET ME SEE IF HE HAS HIS WITS ABOUT HIM.

EACH DAY THE KING WOULD POINT AT THE SUN AND YASHOVARMAN WOULD LEAVE DISAPPOINTED.

BUT ONE DAY —

MAHARAJ, I HAVE BEEN SEEKING ALMS OF YOU FOR A LONG TIME NOW.

I KNOW. BUT THE SUN GOD...

AS THE KING LOOKED UP HE DID NOT SEE THE SUN.

OH!

THERE WAS A TOTAL SOLAR ECLIPSE.

WHATEVER YOU WISH TO GIVE PLEASE GIVE NOW...

...WHEN MY ENEMY IS STILL IN THE GRIP OF HIS ENEMY*

HA! HA!

THE KING REMOVED HIS GOLD NECKLACE AND YASHOVARMAN RECEIVED HIS GIFT AT LAST.

GLORY BE TO YOU, MAHARAJ.

* ACCORDING TO PURANAS AN ECLIPSE IS CAUSED WHEN THE SUN OR THE MOON IS SWALLOWED BY THE DEMONS RAHU OR KETU.